How We Say I Love You

Glossary

Mandarin Chinese to English

Xī fàn (shee fahn) 稀飯: rice porridge

Zǎo ān (tsao ahn) 早安: good morning

Gān miàn (gan myen) 乾麵: dry noodle dish

Jiā yóu (jyah yoh) 加油: a cheer of encouragement; directly translated as "add oil"

Chī fàn le (chee fahn luh) 吃飯了: it's time to eat

Wǎn'ān (wahn ahn) 晚安: good night

Taiwanese Hokkien to English

Ah Gong *agōng* (ah gohng) 阿公: grandfather

Ah Ma *amà* (ah mah) 阿媽: grandmother

How We Say
I Love You

Nicole Chen

illustrated by

Lenny Wen

Alfred A. Knopf · New York

My family loves me,
and I love them.
But we don't use words to say "I love you."

Instead, my mom stirs her love into a pot of steaming xī fàn.
A chorus of "Zǎo ān, Hana" welcomes me to the table,
and we start the day together, our bellies and hearts full.

Ah Gong shows me the love he feels when he walks me to school.
As I hop over cracks, his steps shuffle next to mine,
and we dance to the rhythm of our feet.

How do I show my family my love?

I do my best at school so they can feel proud.

When the teacher asks a question, I raise my hand.

And at recess, I run as fast as I can.
As I catch my breath,
I imagine how bright their eyes will shine
when I tell them how hard I tried.

My tummy rumbles.

I find Ah Ma's gān miàn steaming inside my lunch.

She sprinkles her love onto the noodles she makes for me.

(And sometimes I find a sweet surprise, too!)

At the game, my dad's love echoes in his cheers:

"Jiā yóu, Hana! Go, go, go!"

My legs pump faster and faster—

I miss.

As I sniff by the sidelines,
my dad holds my hand and whispers in my ear.
With his every word, my bravery grows,
and I dash back onto the field to try again.

The moment I get home, I run to find the rest of my family.
Stories from our day spill from our lips,
and we settle into the sweetness of being together again.

Then, as the smells of dinner fill our home,
I rest my head on the belly that holds someone precious and new.
I tell it about things like ice cream and swings and rain,
and the love that's waiting when it joins us.

Dad calls us to the table: "Chī fàn le!"
We show Ah Ma and Ah Gong our love
when we let them fill their bowls first.
They pick the best pieces that will keep them strong.
(Yet those pieces often end up in *my* bowl!)

Finally, as night takes over day,
we say "I love you" with the last things we do.
I rub the knots out of Ah Ma's feet
and pour Ah Gong the tea that helps him sleep.

While my dad and I read side by side,
my mom tucks my sheets in tight.
With their good-night kisses still soft against my cheek,
I whisper a last "Wǎn'ān."

In my family,
our love lives in all the things we do for one another.
That is how we say "I love you."

For my mom and dad. Thank you for all the love
you've shown me over the years. —N.C.

For my parents and siblings, who express their love
through actions rather than words. —L.W.

THIS IS A BORZOI BOOK PUBLISHED BY ALFRED A. KNOPF

Text copyright © 2022 by Nicole Chen
Jacket art and interior illustrations copyright © 2022 by Lenny Wen

All rights reserved. Published in the United States by Alfred A. Knopf, an imprint of
Random House Children's Books, a division of Penguin Random House LLC, New York.

Knopf, Borzoi Books, and the colophon are registered trademarks of Penguin Random House LLC.

Visit us on the Web! rhcbooks.com
Educators and librarians, for a variety of teaching tools, visit us at RHTeachersLibrarians.com

Library of Congress Cataloging-in-Publication Data is available upon request.
ISBN 978-0-593-42839-9 (trade) — ISBN 978-0-593-42840-5 (lib. bdg.) —
ISBN 978-0-593-42841-2 (ebook) —
ISBN 978-0-593-70273-4 (proprietary)

The text of this book is set in 15-point Filson Soft.
The illustrations were created using Photoshop and a graphic tablet.
Book design by Taline Boghosian

MANUFACTURED IN CHINA

December 2022   10 9 8 7 6 5 4 3 2 1   First Edition

This Imagination Library edition is published by Random House Children's Books, a division of Penguin Random House LLC, exclusively
for Dolly Parton's Imagination Library, a not-for-profit program designed to inspire a love of reading and learning, sponsored in part
by The Dollywood Foundation. Penguin Random House's trade editions of this work are available wherever books are sold.